HENRY HECKELBECK

Gets a Dragon

By **Wanda Coven**

Illustrated by **Priscilla Burris**

LITTLE SIMON

New York   London   Toronto   Sydney   New Delhi

This book is a work of fiction. Any references to historical events, real people, or real places are used fictitiously. Other names, characters, places, and events are products of the author's imagination, and any resemblance to actual events or places or persons, living or dead, is entirely coincidental.

LITTLE SIMON

An imprint of Simon & Schuster Children's Publishing Division
1230 Avenue of the Americas, New York, New York, 10020
First Little Simon hardcover edition December 2019
Copyright © 2019 by Simon & Schuster, Inc.
Also available in a Little Simon paperback edition.

For information about special discounts for bulk purchases, please contact Simon & Schuster Special Sales at 1-866-506-1949 or business@simonandschuster.com. The Simon & Schuster Speakers Bureau can bring authors to your live event. For more information or to book an event contact the Simon & Schuster Speakers Bureau at 1-866-248-3049 or visit our website at www.simonspeakers.com.
Designed by Ciara Gay
Manufactured in the United States of America 1119 FFG
10 9 8 7 6 5 4 3 2 1
Library of Congress Cataloging-in-Publication Data
Names: Coven, Wanda, author. | Burris, Priscilla, illustrator.
Title: Henry Heckelbeck gets a dragon / by Wanda Coven ; illustrated by Priscilla Burris.
Description: First Little Simon paperback edition. | New York : Little Simon, [2019] | Series: [Henry Heckelbeck ; 1] | Summary: Future spy Henry discovers that he has magic, like his big sister, Heidi, when he accidentally creates a tiny dragon, which definitely does not belong at Brewster Elementary School.
Identifiers: LCCN 2019017917 | ISBN 9781534461048 (hc) | ISBN 9781534461031 (pbk) | ISBN 9781534461055 (eBook)
Subjects: | CYAC: Magic—Fiction. | Dragons—Fiction. | Schools—Fiction. | Friendship—Fiction. | Brothers and sisters—Fiction.
Classification: LCC PZ7.C83393 Hgg 2019 | DDC [Fic]—dc23
LC record available at https://lccn.loc.gov/2019017917

CONTENTS

Chapter 1

BACK TO SCHOOL

Henry's eyes popped open.

"First day of school!" he cried. He hopped out of bed, fully dressed.

Henry always slept in his clothes. It saved time.

He brushed his teeth with his special two-sided toothbrush. It could reach every tooth.

Then he zipped into the hallway.

Blammo! Henry crashed right into his older sister, Heidi.

"Hey, bub! Watch out next time!" she said.

Henry apologized. "Sorry, sis!"

Then he took off down the stairs. Henry loved his sister, but sometimes she could be a total grump-a-saurus.

Henry slipped into his seat at the table.

Mom gave Henry a strawberry-banana smoothie in a to-go cup. He liked to finish his smoothie on the way to the bus stop. It saved time.

Heidi plunked down at the kitchen table.

"Smoothies?" she complained. "I wanted pancakes."

"Then why don't you turn your smoothie into what you WANT?" Henry suggested.

Heidi looked at Mom.

"No magic at the table,"
Mom said firmly.

Heidi rolled her eyes.

Magic was normal at the
Heckelbeck house.

Heidi was a witch—so were Henry's Mom and Aunt Trudy.

Henry and Dad were regular, everyday people, and Henry was fine with that.

Henry checked the clock and yelled, "Gotta go!"

"Not so fast!" said Dad. "We need a first-day-of-school picture!"

It took a few tries before
they got the best one.

Henry's first day of school
was off to a very normal start.

But today was going to be anything but normal.

That was because Henry Heckelbeck had a secret.

He just didn't know it yet.

Chapter 2

BEST BUDS

Whap! Whap!

Dudley Day slapped the seat beside him on the bus. Henry and Dudley had been best friends ever since they first met.

"Over here!" Dudley cried, whapping the seat again.

Henry plopped into the spot next to Dudley.

They did their secret handshake, which went like this:

Slap high!

Slap low!

Slap side to side!

Elbows!

Fist bump!

Hip bump!

At the end, thumbs-up!

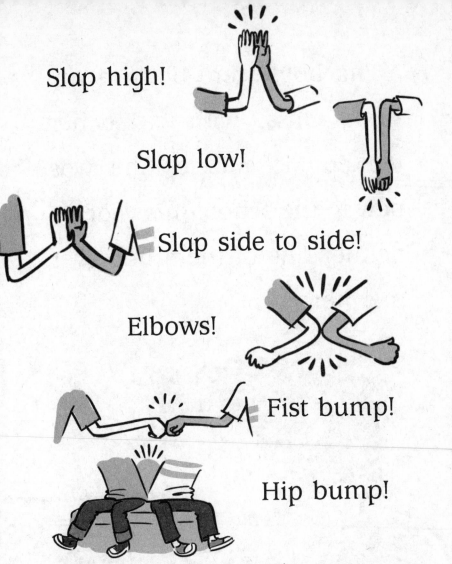

15

The boys were both in the same class, with a teacher named Ms. Mizzle. She was new to the school this year, so neither one of them had ever met her.

"I wonder what she's like?" asked Dudley.

"I did a little detective work over the summer," Henry said. "I learned a few things about the new teacher, and I took notes."

He flipped open his spy notebook.

"'Real name: Miranda Mizzle. Likes: flowers, gardening, science, math, and wearing yellow hats. Dislikes: kids wiping noses on their sleeves, bullies.'"

Dudley raised his eyebrows. "Where did you get all the info?"

"My mom," Henry said. "She's in a hiking club with Ms. Mizzle. Oh, and one time I saw Ms. Mizzle wearing a yellow hat."

Dudley nodded. He was impressed.

"So do you think she's a homework robot?" Dudley asked.

Henry shrugged. "Well, I know that she's not a robot. But also my mom says that Ms. Mizzle will only assign GOOD homework."

Dudley scrunched his face.
"What?! But there's NO such
thing as GOOD homework!"

Henry laughed. "At least we're in the same class, so we will have the same homework!"

Dudley held out his fist, and Henry bumped it, best-friend style.

Chapter 3

IN THE BAG

Ms. Mizzle stood in front of the class. She didn't have on her yellow hat, but she *did* have on a yellow dress.

Henry wrote in his notebook, *Likes yellow*.

It was very important to get spy information right.

He also noted an empty desk in his classroom. Was a student missing? Maybe that was another mystery he could solve.

"Welcome to the first day of school!" their new teacher said in a cheery voice.

Ms. Mizzle talked about their classroom rules and introduced the class guinea pig, named Lil' Ham.

Then she held up a stack of brown paper bags.

"Does anyone know what we might do with these bags?" Ms. Mizzle asked.

Henry raised his hand. "Put stuff in them?"

"Exactly," she said. "Do you know what *kind* of stuff?"

The class guessed things like candy and bugs.

"Those are all *good* guesses," she said. "These bags are for a special project called All About Me. It works like this."

Ms. Mizzle held up a gardening glove, a book, and a tiny boot on a key chain.

"What do these things tell you about me?" she asked.

A girl with pigtails raised her
hand. "You like to garden?"

"Yes!" said Ms. Mizzle.

"You like to read!" said a boy
with glasses.

"And you like to HIKE!" Dudley said. He already knew this from Henry's spy list.

"Very good!" the teacher said. "Tonight I want everyone to find three things that tell us something about *you*."

Dudley raised his hand and waved it in the air. "May I put my soccer ball in the bag?"

Ms. Mizzle opened an empty
bag and showed it to the class.

"Only bring things that fit in
the bag," she said.

A girl in a pink top raised
her hand.

"What about brand-new baby hamsters?" she said. "They are REALLY small and REALLY cute, and they would REALLY love to visit school."

Ms. Mizzle shook her head and said, "Let's leave pets at home. If you want to include them, be creative. You could draw a picture of your baby hamsters instead."

Then somebody opened the classroom door. Everyone turned to see a kid dressed in jeans, a T-shirt, and a baseball cap.

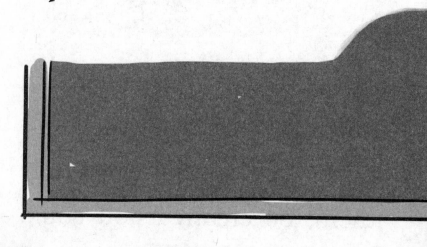

"Class, today we have a new student at our school," said Ms. Mizzle. "This is Mackenzie Maplethorpe. Mackenzie just moved to Brewster."

Henry wrote in his spy notebook, *New kid in class. Empty-desk mystery solved.*

Mackenzie pulled off her baseball cap. Her long hair tumbled down.

"I go by Max," she said.

Henry knew a girl named Melanie Maplethorpe. She was in his sister's class. Max wasn't like Melanie as far as Henry could tell.

"Now let's give Max a Brewster Elementary hello!" Ms. Mizzle cheered.

"Hello, Max!" the class sang.

But the new girl didn't say hello back.

Chapter 4

THREE THINGS

The first day of school zoomed by. Henry and Dudley counted coins in math. In science they dropped things in water to see what would float and what would sink to the bottom.

They had chicken nuggets
and rainbow yogurt sticks for
lunch. Then they played tag
at recess.

"I love school," Henry said
on the bus back home.

"Me too!" Dudley agreed.
"I'm not sure that new girl
liked it."

Henry nodded. "Hmm, Max didn't have a partner in math," he said.

"She ate lunch all by herself," Dudley added.

"Then, at recess, she just WATCHED everyone," Henry said as he made a note of all these things.

"Maybe the new girl wished Ms. Mizzle WAS a homework robot," Dudley said.

Henry laughed. "Maybe," he said. "We'll find out more about Max when she does her All About Me project."

The ride back went by fast, and soon the bus was at Henry's stop.

Henry waved good-bye to Dudley. Then he ran all the way home and went straight to his room.

Henry held his All About Me bag and looked around.

Hmm, he thought. *What three things best describe ME?*

He found his magnifying glass on the carpet.

"Well, first of all, I'm a secret spy," he said, and plopped the magnifying glass into his paper bag.

"Hey! I also love soccer." Henry grabbed his goalie gloves from a drawer in his dresser.

"Now I just need ONE more thing." Henry hunted through his toy chest.

There were stuffed animals, but nothing seemed right.

Then he turned to his bookshelf. On the very top he spied his mini remote-controlled dragon.

"That's IT!" he cried.

The toy dragon would be perfect. It had eyes that lit up. It could also roll its head, roar, and fly in a circle.

I wonder how it got way up there, Henry thought.

The dragon was leaning against an old book—a book that had been sitting on his shelf forever.

Henry had to find a way to get his dragon down.

Chapter 5

THE WEIRD OLD BOOK

Henry dragged a chair over and climbed onto it. The toy dragon was still too high.

He put one foot on the shelf and reached for the dragon again.

He could barely poke the toy
with his fingertips.

And that's when his door
opened.

"HENRY!" shouted his sister.
"GET DOWN!"

Henry lost his balance and rolled onto the carpet like an action hero.

Things from the bookcase
tumbled down. The old book
landed in front of him.

"HENRY! You could have
gotten hurt!" Heidi cried.

Henry rubbed his head and
smiled.

"I was fine until you scared me," he said.

"I'm serious!" Heidi went on. "The bookshelf could have fallen on you!"

Henry had never thought of that.

"You better pick things up before Mom gets home," Heidi added.

Then she marched out of the room and shut the door behind her.

Henry pulled his dragon out of the mess. Luckily, nothing was broken.

Suddenly a hum sounded in the room. It was coming from the old book on the floor.

Henry touched the book, and it began to glow.

"Whoa!" whispered Henry.

Chapter 6

THE DRAGON SPELL

Henry opened the glowing book.

Something hard landed in his lap with a clunk. It looked like his gold soccer medal.

It had the letter *M* on it.

Henry put the medal around his neck.

Suddenly the pages of the book were turning on their own. Finally they stopped on a picture of a dragon.

"Cool!" Henry exclaimed.

Then the page turned, and a voice from nowhere read the book aloud.

How to Get a Dragon

Have you ever wanted your very own pet dragon? A dragon that would follow you to school? Or one that would play with you? And sleep on your bed at night? If you really want a dragon, then this is the spell for you!

Ingredients:
1 picture of your favorite dragon
1 tablespoon of hot sauce
1 cup of water
2 teaspoons of baking soda

Mix the ingredients together in a bowl. Hold your medallion in one hand and place your other hand over the bowl. Chant the following spell.

Dragon soar!
And dragon dive!

Make my dragon come ALIVE!

Note: Dragon training not included.

Magic! It was magic! Henry could not believe it.

He got the ingredients faster than a dragon could breathe fire.

Then he mixed them together,
took off the medallion, and held
it while he chanted the spell.

There was a puff of smoke,
and Henry looked around his
room.

It should have been easy to
find a real live dragon.

But Henry could not see one anywhere.

It didn't work, Henry thought. *Maybe I'm just a normal kid after all.*

He put the medallion back inside the book.

Henry picked up his toy dragon and said, "You're still great, even if you aren't real."

He put the toy into his bag
and started cleaning his room.

Chapter 7

FIRE-BREATHING FREAK-OUT!

The next morning Henry's bag felt heavier than it had the night before.

That's odd, Henry thought.

He peeked inside.

Magnifying glass. *Check.*

Goalie gloves. *Check.*

Dragon toy. *Check.*

Nothing had changed.

When the bus came, Henry
sat next to Dudley.

"What's in your All About
Me bag?" Henry asked.

Dudley smiled. He pulled
out a stinky soccer cleat.

Next, he pulled out a pack of
sour candy. Dudley loved sour
candy.

And lastly, he held up his
light-up yo-yo.

"Those are great!" Henry said.

"Okay, so what did YOU bring?" Dudley asked.

Henry opened his bag. The magnifying glass and the goalie gloves were there, but the dragon was *missing*.

"Oh no!" Henry cried. "My dragon is GONE!"

There was a hole in the bottom of his bag—only it wasn't just any hole. The bag had been scorched.

Chapter 8

SPY VS. SPY

"Don't worry. I'll help you find your toy dragon!" Dudley said. "It's not like it ran away."

The bus parked at school, and the boys waited for everyone to leave.

Dudley checked the front of the bus. Henry crawled toward the back. There, he spied his very real dragon.

He dove for it, but the dragon was fast. It flew out an open window.

Henry tried the remote control, but it didn't work.

"WOW!" Dudley cried. "I didn't know your dragon could fly like THAT!"

"Neither did I!" Henry admitted as he raced off the bus.

As Henry chased his toy, he
ran smack into Max.

She dropped her All About
Me bag and something rolled
out. It was a magnifying glass
just like his!

Max grabbed it and shoved it back into her bag.

"Watch where you're going!" she said.

"You should be careful too!" he said, but Max was already gone.

91

Chapter 9

THE WHAT-IFS

Henry couldn't decide which was worse, missing one of his All About Me items or having his real magic dragon loose in the classroom.

He squirmed in his chair.

What if the dragon lands in Ms. Mizzle's hair? What if the dragon tries to eat all the kids' snacks? Or WHAT IF the dragon burns down the WHOLE classroom?!

Then Dudley nudged Henry's foot and said, "Somebody's staring at you."

Somebody *was* staring at him. But it wasn't a dragon. It was Max!

She pointed behind Henry.

He turned around.

A tiny toy dragon sat on top of his cubby.

Henry carefully raised his hand. He did not want to scare the dragon away. He also did not want the class to see the dragon.

"Ms. Mizzle, may I please get something from my backpack?"

His teacher nodded.

Henry walked to his backpack with his best there's-no-dragon-on-top-of-my-cubby walk.

With every step Henry took, the little dragon tilted its head and flashed its red eyes playfully.

With a gulp, Henry reached for the dragon, but it flew away and Henry fell into the wall of cubbies.

Backpacks, jackets, and snacks tumbled onto the floor. The whole class laughed. At least, almost the whole class.

One student did not laugh at all: *Max*. She had seen Henry's very real dragon escape out the window.

Chapter 10

IT'S ONLY A TOY

The day moved slowly. All Henry could think about was finding the dragon.

Even after the cubby mess, Henry kept looking. But he didn't see anything.

Luckily, Henry made it to recess without being called on to share his All About Me bag.

He slipped on his soccer gloves and grabbed his trusty magnifying glass. It was time for a dragon hunt.

He tiptoed around the swing
set and monkey bars. Then he
spied tiny dragon paw prints.

He followed the tracks. They
led to an old oak tree.

Suddenly the dragon peeked out from the branches. It looked scared.

Henry gave a little wave and the dragon flew down to him.

He quickly cupped his hands
around the dragon when it
landed. He felt the small wings
beat against his soccer gloves.

He looked at the dragon for
the first time up close.

"You are SO cute," Henry
told the dragon, "but I don't

think Brewster Elementary is the best place for dragons."

The dragon's eyes flashed in agreement. It was listening to him.

Henry took a deep breath and said, "I WISH you were a TOY dragon again."

KA-ZING! A small glow like the one from the book surrounded the dragon. It instantly turned back into a toy.

"Wow!" Henry said aloud, just as somebody tapped him on the shoulder.

It was Max.

"You better tell me what's going on," she said.

Henry was nervous. Had Max seen anything?

"What do you mean?" he asked.

Max pointed at his dragon. "I saw that thing FLY," she said.

Henry took off his gloves and pulled out the remote control.

"It does fly," he said. "But it's ONLY a toy."

Then he made the dragon fly in a circle.

"See?" he said. "By the way, I'm Henry Heckelbeck, Private Eye and Super Spy. I noticed you're a detective too." He showed her his magnifying glass.

Max reached into her All About Me bag and showed Henry *her* magnifying glass too.

"Maybe we can solve a mystery together sometime," Henry suggested.

A half smile spread across Max's face.

"Maybe," she said as the bell rang. "Because there is definitely something weird going on at this school."

Henry knew Max was right. *There WAS something weird going on here.* And Henry Heckelbeck was on the case.

Check out the next book starring

HeNRY HeCKELBECK

HeNRY HeCKELBECK
Never Cheats

Henry Heckelbeck pulled a round sandwich out of his lunch box. Mom had made it with a cookie cutter. Henry showed his best friend, Dudley.

"What does THIS look like?"

An excerpt from *Henry Heckelbeck Never Cheats*